This is the story
of Nina Rose
who loved to dance
on the tips of her toes.

Each Monday at ballet
through the studio door,
she saw big girls *en pointe*
with their toes to the floor.

Nina thought to herself,
with a very long sigh:
"If **they** can do that,
then why can't I?"

When their class finished
and Nina's began,
she went up on her toes
and in she ran.

With toes curled under
and heels held high,
Nina Rose felt as if
she could reach the sky.

Miss Julie said firmly,
"Nina Rose, not yet!
You'll damage your feet
and get very upset.

You're the lead in our concert
just two days away,
so look after your feet.
Off your toes you must stay.

When you are older,
you'll have *pointe* shoes too;
however for now,
demi *pointe* must do."

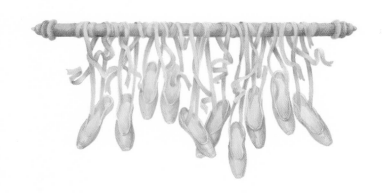

At home her Mother
kept telling her, "No!"
But spinning away
Nina Rose would go.

She covered her ears
not listening at all,
and pranced on her toes
right down the front hall.

With teeth gritted tight,
Nina tried to ignore
the pain in her toes;
they were getting so sore.

Harry

Nina

Charlie

10

As she marked her height
on the kitchen wall,
her brothers shrieked,
"You're not that tall!"

"Why"… groaned Harry,
"does Nina Rose
have to do **everything**
up on her toes?"

"We've tried to warn her,"
Mother said.
"Now quickly children,
off to bed."

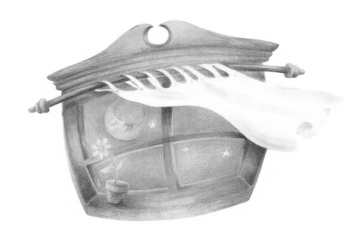

As Nina was climbing
up the stairs,
the pain in her toes
became hard to bear.

They hurt and ached,
she started to cry;
"Dad, could you help me?
These stairs seem so… high."

"Of course," he replied,
"but I strongly suggest,
that now you lie down
and get some rest!"

She bathed her feet
and kept them high.
Tick-Tock, Tick-Tock...
the time crawled by.

All Nina could do
was to hope and pray
she'd be able to dance
by the following day.

At the final rehearsal
she tried to be strong,
but Miss Julie could see
that something was wrong.

She said gently to Nina,
"I am sorry to say,
I'm giving your role
to Amy to play.

If only you'd listened
to Mother and me,
you'd have saved yourself
from this misery."

Nina fought back the tears
as she sat in despair,
while her very best friend
jumped high in the air.

With *sautés* and *jetés*
and *pas de deux*,
Amy practised the part
that was meant for her!

On the night of the concert
Nina felt even sadder
as they hoisted her up
to the top of a ladder!

Her toes still hurt,
so all she could be
was the angel on top
of the Christmas tree.

Girls glided by
like sunlit clouds…
In pink *pointe* shoes
they looked so proud.

"Oh"… Nina sighed
from the top of the tree,
"I hope one day
that will be me."

Then something caught
her eye below.
Amy had forgotten
which way to go!

Like a deer with the light
in its eyes, she froze...
She could only stare blankly
down at her toes.

23

A sudden hush
came over the stage.
The pianist repeated
the notes on her page.

All eyes were on Amy,
so lost and so small…
When there came from above
a gentle call.

Words floating down
like flakes of snow:
"Glissade. Jeté.
Quick! Off you go."

Amy's head lifted up.
She came out of her trance.
Fear melted away,
and once more she could dance!

Nina guided her friend
like a puppet with strings,
until she was dancing
as if she had wings.

From then to the end
there was hardly a pause
as Amy performed
to delighted applause.

Curtsies were taken
and flowers were thrown…
but poor Nina Rose
felt all on her own.

After the show…
silent and glum,
she went to sit
beside her Mum.

"Now my darling,
don't despair;
in the end
you will get there.

Practise hard,
but keep it slow;
step by step
is the way to go."

Her excited friends
all gathered around,
but still Nina Rose
didn't make a sound.

They called her
their beautiful angel above.
Miss Julie just nodded
and smiled with love.

"Oh Nina," said Amy,
"you're my very best friend.
Once you showed me the way
I could dance to the end.

All of these flowers
should belong to you…
My guardian angel
who guided me through."

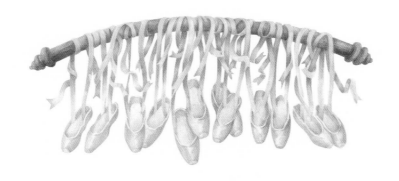

"No Amy… they're yours.
I've learnt the hard way,
that until I am ready,
off my toes I must stay.

Just one rose to remind me…
When all is not right,
don't ever give up,
there's a rainbow in sight.

Let's make a wish
that in next year's show,
we'll dance side by side
in the very front row."

Amy hugged her and waved
as she skipped away…
a wonderful end
to a troublesome day.

That night Nina Rose
had the sweetest of dreams.
She was spinning and leaping
through meadows and streams.

With *pirouettes*, *jetés*
and magical poses,
ending deep in a curtsey…
surrounded by roses.

Ballet Terms

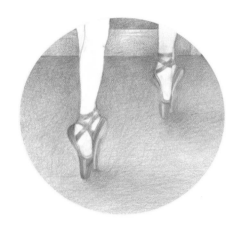

En (on) Pointe
To dance on the tips of the toes in *pointe* shoes.

Pointe shoes
Special ballet shoes with a firm sole and block toe for extra support when dancers are *en pointe*.
Three senior girls *en pointe* in *pointe* shoes.

Demi pointe
Half point – standing on the ball of the foot.
Amy is on *demi pointe*.

Pas de deux (pah-de-der)
Steps for two people dancing together.
Amy and her partner are practising a *pas de deux*.

Sauté (so-tay)

Jump – with pointed toes. Amy is rehearsing a *sauté*.

Jeté (jeh-tay)

Throw – extend the leg strongly and jump onto it. Nina dreams she leaps high into the air with a *grand jeté* (grahn jeh-tay) – big throw.

Glissade (gliss-ahd)

Glide from one foot to the other.

Pirouette (pir-oo-ett)

Spin – on one leg.
In her dream Nina Rose spins in a *pirouette en pointe*.

Pointe Work

Following many years of training, after the age of 11 or 12, your ballet teacher will advise and guide you as to whether your body is strong enough to dance *en pointe*.

To darling Nina, Harry, Charlie and my ballet students over the years

who were the inspiration for this story.

All my thanks to family and friends who contributed in so many wonderful ways.

First Published in Australia 2004, by Sassey Pty Ltd.
Ph: 61 (08) 93224144 Fax: 61 (08) 9322 5918
email: office@caperangewireless.com

Copyright © Sandra Wise 2004
Text Sandra Wise A.R.A.D.
Illustrations Lina Linton

The National Library of Australia CIP data

Wise, Sandra.
Nina Rose's Toes.
For primary-school aged children.
ISBN 0-9752076-1-X
I. Ballerinas – Juvenile fiction. I. Linton, Lina.
II. Title.

A823.4

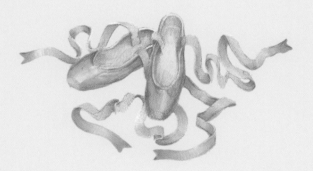